Bridges
101

gas pumps,
banana bread,
and other
attitudes

Bridges
101

Ruthie Jacobsen

Ruthie Jacobsen, *author*

Bryan Gray, *cover & content design*

Don Jacobsen, *editor*

Cover photo copyright © Angel Herrero de Frutos

ISBN 978-0-615-21106-0

PRINTED IN U.S.A.

Table of Contents

Prologue

The
kingdom
advances
among
friends

Introduction

Why we think you're going to want to read this book...

I don't know for sure of course, but this may be one of the most liberating books you've ever read.

No, this isn't all there is to witnessing. Maybe it's more like pre-witnessing. Maybe it's more like earning the right to tell our story. Let's call it a healthy incursion into the 1st angel's message of Revelation 14 which invites men and women to fall in love with the Creator God so they are drawn "to worship Him."

If this were being written as a college textbook, it might be for a class called Contagious 101.

This book is for "the rest of us," the non-Mark Finleys and non-Walter Pearsons among us, who get sweaty palms every time a witnessing opportunity appears, for fear we'll...well, just for fear.

This is a fresh route to happy for those who harbor a Spirit-led longing but who kick themselves because they never quite get up the courage.

This is church outside the box. Ambitious promises. Some new kinds of bridges. You can *do* this.

Chapter 1

A Bathroom Party?

If you're going to do a bathroom remodel, no matter what they tell you, you can just know that it will take twice as long and cost twice as much. But God can use even that to generate the interest of neighbors and workers. God will use *anything* to reach those He loves, and when He owns the house it just gives Him another tool.

Our ailing master bath had some serious problems—worn carpet on the floor, a tiny triangular shaped shower, and pinkish-mauve-colored bathtub and fixtures for starters! It was depressing just to walk into the little bathroom. So we contacted some people who were the "pros" and launched into a major renovation.

We made some interesting discoveries as we prayed for guidance. God sent us some wonderful people who not only knew just what to do, but who tackled every task with an eye for beauty and convenience. They were pleased too, with the way it was all coming together.

And something happened we hadn't anticipated—we got acquainted with a bunch of people we would never have met in any other way. We learned about their families, their beliefs, and their needs. We listened as they told us about their life stories and it was unmistakable to us that as they were at work, so was God.

Midway through the project we invited our cabinet man, Phil, to come to church and tell his story of how God had brought him from a life of liquor, drugs, dishonesty, and immorality, to deliverance and peace. We met his wife and family and watched the pride in their eyes.

The members of our little church wept with Phil as he told his story and praised God for His deliverance. We probably would never have met Phil or heard his story if he hadn't come into our home to help us.

As the bathroom work neared completion, several times someone would say, "I'd love to see this when it's finished." Or a neighbor would say, "It's been fun, watching the progress, even seeing your bathtub out on the deck. We wondered if you going to have a new place to bathe." More and more people were asking about what the bathroom would look like when all the dust had settled.

Some of the workers who were part of the project would even say things like, "My wife never gets to see my finished work. She'd love to see this."

Because we took a walk-in closet and made it into a shower, and then made a large window in the shower, they wanted to see it when it was done. (By the way, we live on a mountainside, and have lots of privacy, in case you were worried.)

So, we decided to have a "Bathroom Party" and invite everyone who had worked on it, their families, our neighbors, and anyone else who wanted to come. We prayed about it at every step, because we sensed that God was doing something rather out of the ordinary here.

We assembled some white plastic "favor bags" ready for each one to take home as they left—with soap, shampoo, toothpaste, shower cap, pens, mouthwash, lotion, and some goodies. Each one had "Jacobsen's Bathroom Party," and the date penned on the side. We wanted them to have a little reminder of the evening.

Incidentally, the items in the bags were donated by the local Holiday Inn manager, who ended up inviting herself to the party. She said that a Bathroom Party would be a first for her. We said it was a first for us, too.

Just before the people came, we again gave the evening to God, asking Him to show us how He would have us touch each person individually for His glory.

As people arrived there was a happy, friendly atmosphere. But also some uncertainty. I mean, what do you *do* at a bathroom party? As they came in, our guests went straight to the bathroom. It was really noisy in there. At one time there were seven people in the shower (no, the water wasn't running).

More than twenty-five showed up that night—all non-members— and what a perfect evening! Even the hummingbirds came and put on a show. There must have been twenty of them darting about and eating from the deck feeders. Apparently they had never seen a bathroom party, either.

After the inspection of the bathroom, we went downstairs for the appetizers, and the blessing. As we stood in a circle we introduced each one and again thanked them for the beautiful job they had done. Then Don prayed, and asked God to bless each of them—and their businesses.

Our neighbor, Pat, came to me after the prayer and said, "Ruthie, I've never seen anything like this before, and I don't think these workers have either."

It was a simple meal—I had prepared four vegetarian entrees, which they quickly devoured. We decided to add a few "bathroom touches" to carry out the theme of the party, so the red juice in the punchbowl had a little sign that said, "Bubble Bath." A bowl of sour cream had a card that said "Shaving Soap." The dessert had some miniature tools on top. The center piece (which someone had sent us) was a roll of toilet paper with a big red bow.

As Melissa and Matt, from the Glass Shop downtown were leaving, she gave me a big hug, and said, "Ruthie, can we do something like this again soon? I want to stay in touch with you." We see Melissa often now, and have prayed with her. They've become good friends. Their 15-year old son calls me Grandma Ruthie.

As Louisa and Sandro (some of our quiet Italian neighbors) were

"Jesus was everywhere here tonight"

leaving after the party that evening, they made the comment: "You didn't say much about it, but Jesus was everywhere here tonight." We looked at each other in amazement and gratitude, knowing that He had orchestrated the entire evening.

Another couple—Phil and Lucille, (the man with the cabinet business)—have come to our home for several different events since then, and have asked us to come to their new, beautiful place of business. They have just had their Grand Opening, and Phil, said, "I want you and Don to come and bless our new place." God is still opening doors and opening hearts, through—if you can believe it—a Bathroom Party.

Now, a bathroom party may not be appropriate for you, but it can be anything that you think of—any excuse to invite people to your home. The fellowship room at your church may be ever so warm and attractive, but most people would rather put their feet under *your* table.

Take any excuse to get together—your non-member friends and neighbors will appreciate it more than you can know. When we pray about it, and give it to God, it becomes Kingdom Business, and He does things in His own way that we might never have even thought of. Isn't it amazing to watch Him? He can take even simple events and turn them into occasions of eternal significance. That's His grace.

Someone has said that a loaf of bread doesn't have two ends, it has two beginnings! What a great attitude. Every day is a new beginning, an opportunity to find someone who needs Him. Maybe a loaf of banana bread, a bottle of water, a smile, a kind word is all that it will take to lift someone's spirits, bring them new hope, and open their hearts to hear what He wants to say to them.

So here's an important prayer we can pray together: "Dear God, please open my eyes; give me a sensitive heart to know how I can respond to Your coaching and just love people as You would. I may not feel very comfortable leading out in neighborhood Bible studies, or going door-to-door down an unfamiliar street, but I can love people. I can love the people You love. I can love the neighbors You have providentially given me, for Your glory. I don't need a bathroom remodeled right now, but I know You'll help me find other creative ways to live loving among them as Jesus did. Thank You, Lord. I'm honored to be on Your team. Amen."

Chapter 2

A New Look At Bridges

Do you believe that God is earnestly seeking to enter the heart of every man, woman, and child on this planet? Is it true?

Another question: What approach is most likely to capture the attention of the non-believer, and the very secular society around us?

Is this true: The message of the gospel must be spoken and also *shown* to the watching world.

Is it true that we need to search for greater effectiveness in our desire to tell His story?

Do you believe that even our great message doesn't help much unless we have an audience who is listening? Is it true?

Do you believe we need to pray daily for the Holy Spirit to help us notice the specific needs of the people around us?

Do practical acts of kindness work as a demonstration of God's love? Is this true?

In Steve Sjogren's great book, "Conspiracy of Kindness," he asks some of these thought-provoking questions.

Do you remember what Jesus said about that? You may wish to refresh your memory by reading Matthew 10:42. He says that *a cup of cold water* given to one of His humblest children will be rewarded.

Steve Sjogren tells a story that will answer many of these questions for us. This incident happened in Cincinnati, Ohio, not long ago.

Joe Delaney, and his 8-year old son, Jared, were playing catch in the backyard, but Joe could see that Jared was thinking about other things. Joe tried to interest him in talking about the Cincinnati Reds, since Jared loved baseball and was a big Reds fan. But Jared seemed distracted by bigger issues that were swirling through his 8-year old mind.

Finally, Jared asked. "Dad, is there a God?"

Joe thought a minute and shrugged his shoulders. "I really don't know, Jared," his dad admitted, "I've never really known much about God." He tried to resume their game, but Jared was still distracted.

"Well, if there is a God, how could we know about Him, and how would He talk to us?" With that, Jared dropped the ball and ran into the house, calling over his shoulder, "I'll be right back."

He returned a few minutes later with three helium balloons left over from his birthday party the previous day, some tape, and a little card. On the card he wrote, "God, if you are real, and You are up there, please send us someone who knows you. Jared." He taped the card to one of the balloons and the boy and his dad watched as they sailed into the blue sky.

It was only a couple of days later that the two of them were driving down a street near their home when they saw a man holding a big sign that read: "CAR WASH—ABSOLUTELY FREE." Jared said, "Dad, we need a car wash; let's try it." So Joe drove in.

Steve Sjogren, the young pastor involved in the free car wash, was on the driver's side of the car, and as Joe's car pulled up the two began talking. Pastor Steve saw Joe reach for his wallet, and heard him say, "I know you're raising money for something, and I appreciate the car wash. We'll be glad to help you with your project."

"No, sir, this is *free*. We don't accept money. We are just washing cars," Steve answered.

"But why would you wash cars for free?" Joe asked.

"Well, we're just showing God's love in a practical way," Pastor Steve replied with a smile.

Joe asked, "Wait a minute, are you guys Christians?"

"Yes, we are." Steve replied.

"Well, are you the kind of Christians that believe in God?" Joe queried.

"We believe in God." Steve had to smile at the question.

Jared lit up. "Dad! God got His mail!" he exclaimed.

Joe told the pastor the story of the helium balloons. Pastor Steve realized again that acts of service with no strings attached, get people's attention.

"God got His mail!"

Now Jared was convinced, and this was the beginning of a new discovery and a new journey for their family.

Do you believe that *anyone* can do simple acts of kindness? Mary Jones, a senior member in our church in Blairsville, Georgia, goes to one of the Methodist Churches in town every Sunday and takes care of their nursery. They love her. We met some folks from that church a few days ago, and they were sure Mary was an "angel." One lady told us about how, some years before, Mary had noticed an unexpected change in the weather coming and brought over some sweaters and coats and warm food for her neighbors. She said, "She didn't know us, but she was so sweet and kind...I'll just never forget her."

Is it true that an *experience* of love often opens a person's heart to a *message* of love? When we moved to Hiawassee, Georgia, we knew no one in our little town, but we soon got acquainted. We took banana bread and brownies and other goodies to our neighbors, and we were always warmly received.

One week when I was to speak at our church, I decided to invite these same non-members to church with us, and then to our home for lunch. Eleven came for church. One more joined us for the lunch, but I count her as number twelve because all through the meal she was getting parts of the sermon from those who had been there.

Another time when there were seven or eight who came for church, we stood in a circle after the service and prayed together. Each time I have invited non-members, they come to me after the service, and often with tears in their eyes and hugs of gratitude, they thank me for inviting them to our church.

Is it a fact that true acts of service go before God as worship? I believe that we are worshiping Him when we are serving those for whom Christ died, and He unites with us to make the experience meaningful to those He loves so much.

Is it true that our acts of ministry and service can actually help to overcome the church-credibility gap which many unbelievers have?

When your acts of kindness begin with prayer, they often find ready acceptance. God Himself reaches hearts with His healing comfort.

A lady in Cincinnati was surprised to discover a little card on her windshield when she rushed back from her shopping. She was concerned because she knew that the time had expired on her parking meter. Would she find a parking ticket?

When she picked up the card she read, "Your parking meter looked hungry, so we fed it. Just showing God's love in a practical way." She later told the pastor that when she read the card, she cried. It was her birthday, and everyone had forgotten. Her husband didn't remember, her children had forgotten. She said, "Everyone forgot...but God."

"Your parking meter looked hungry"

God says that He is the one who devises means to call His children to Himself (2 Samuel 14:14b, NIV). He is creative. He knows just what will work to reach the heart. And when we go on His errands He is the one who puts in our hearts ways by which we can be attractive extensions of His hands.

An important distinction here: We can do "nice" things for others —but that's doing things on the human level; those are common social graces. It might make me feel good to be nice to someone, but that's not the goal.

With prayer and the presence of the Holy Spirit, you'll be led to acts of *kindness*. These are the generous gifts of your time and interest done purely for *their* benefit. This is why it is especially vital to remember who we are representing because it is "the kindness of God that leads... to repentance." (Romans 2:4 NIV)

God has promised to go before us and open the way. He even makes it fun, and *His* presence, mixed with *our* kindness, can change a life— for eternity.

Chapter 3

Low-Risk/High-Grace

Ever hear the term, low-risk/high-grace? We hadn't either, but the more we lived with it the more we came to see it as one of those statements that kind of sneaks up on you, and you find yourself saying, "Why didn't I think of that before?" It's a term we borrowed from our friend, Steve Sjogren, and it is jam-packed with meaning.

By definition, low-risk/high-grace is any Kingdom witnessing activity that is comfortable for the timid but has the muscle to make a powerful grace statement. It's a love-sharing activity that is doable even for those who have never seen themselves as members of the God Squad.

Most anyone can give away a bottle of cold water. This process doesn't have to be complicated. Jesus asked us to do simple things: visit those in prison, give clothing when needed, food to the hungry. These are not difficult assignments. He doesn't ask us to do difficult things— just share His love in simple ways. Jesus knew that those simple things have the capacity to change lives.

This insight was so important to Jesus that He explains to us how

He will separate those on His right from those on His left. (Matthew 25:34-40) As you read that passage be sure to note how He identifies those on His right who are faithful in their ministry.

It is not accidental that He says nothing about their willingness to go to foreign countries to do ministry. It was not an inadvertent omission that He doesn't mention their ability to preach? Was it the slip of an editor's pen that He doesn't require that His followers be skilled in the production of hope-filled books? Does He request that they perform great miracles? No, He tells them that they've been faithful when they have done the little things, the kindnesses shown to others in need. The low-risk/high-grace stuff.

While the simple things we do may not register as terribly significant or make the evening news, the fact is that this kind of service may well be noted in heaven as an activity of "high grace" because God is so desperate to find those who will continue what His Son did when He was here.

Let me tell you a wonderful story about a growing church, a church in Loganville, Georgia, just outside of Atlanta. Sjogren would call these people "seed-flingers." Great term.

A small group of our friends got together to plant a church in a city where there had never been a Seventh-day Adventist Church. They looked for all kinds of outreach opportunities that would put them in touch with their unchurched neighbors, that would build bridges.

Let me give you a sample... The town of Loganville has an annual "LoganFest"celebration. Among the booths of crafts, local foods, music and fun, Pam and Steve Reifsnyder, with Ted and Sharon Winslow, Chris and Troy Jenkins, and others, set up a booth where they gave out bottles of water. Bottles of water! That doesn't take a lot of theological training.

Attached to each bottle was a little card that said simply:

Yes. . . It really is FREE!
We hope this small gift brightens your day.
It's a simple way of saying that God loves you.
Let us know *if we can be of more assistance.*

On the other side of the card was the name and address of the church, their web site, and time of services.

Now, you and I have walked around at enough County Fairs in August to know that a drink of cool water is a very welcome gift. Simple. Inexpensive. Low-risk.

But you can hear the questions, can't you: "Why would these folks do this for free when they could sell them? What's the catch?" The card answers the question. Something about, "It's a simple way of saying that God loves you." High grace.

So, what's happening? The church is growing, right? In fact, bursting at the seams. It began with twelve members in Jeremy and Jennifer Reifsnyder's home (Steve and Pam's son), and then grew to a large enough group they needed to rent a church—which they later purchased. Now they are planning to enlarge the sanctuary to hold all of those who show up for worship.

God has provided funds, seating, and kind non-member friends to meet their every need. We were there with them just yesterday. What a great experience to see Jenny and Klinton, (Steve and Pam's daughter and son-in-law) leading out in the Sabbath services, welcoming the worshipers. It's been a family project, with the Reifsnyders, Winslows, and others, and God insists on showing up. In the five years since launch, they have gone from twelve to 142 members. Recently they planted *another* new church in Monroe, Georgia, nearby. You see, the book of Acts is still being written.

The week before our visit, the two churches completed a Revelation Seminar and baptized eleven, with more still in preparation.

Invest

and

invite

We have a friend whose church's theme is: Invest and Invite. The pastor says, "You build the friendship, invest in the friend, invite them over, take them on a picnic, do things together. When the situation is right, invite them to church and we'll introduce them to Jesus."

Sounds to me like a great way to build a bridge.

Using low-risk/high-grace activities, we've discovered, helps solve the recruiting problem, too. People like to be a part of something that helps others. They are often eager to be involved in acts of love. Last Christmas Franklin Graham's organization, Samaritan's Purse*, sent 7.75 million "shoe boxes" to needy children all over the world in his Operation ChristmasChild Project. Have you heard of it?

Each box is gender- and age-specific, and includes items like articles of clothing, toys, school supplies, and candy. The boxes are sent at Christmastime to children who are desperately needy.

Last November, we discovered we had only two weeks before the deadline for the boxes to be filled. They have to be shipped early in November because many have long distances to travel.

We circulated letters to our neighbors and other friends in our little town, inviting them to prepare boxes. Then we had to be away for two weeks.

When we returned, we discovered that the word had indeed gotten around and our neighbors and friends were looking forward to our "Box Party." We had told them that if they didn't finish a complete box, just to bring the contents and come to the party with their items, and

*You can make contact with Samaritan's Purse at www.operationchristmaschild.org.

we'd finish the packing.

When we finished that evening, there were a total of 52 boxes from our "party." Each box was prayed over and lovingly packed. The next morning they would be taken to a collection site and from there shipped all over the world.

We served soup and sandwiches and cookies, because it was, after all, advertised as a "party." And there was a warm spirit present. We have a happy photo of all the smiling faces. Later we sent out a thank-you note to all those who had worked so hard and fast, with a copy of the photo as a reminder of all the fun. They loved it.

But one of the surprises for us came at the end of the evening when several told us, "Any time you're doing something for others who are needy, please contact us. We want to be part of it." Some commented that it gave them a good feeling to be working together as a team, knowing that it would make a difference to a little kid in need somewhere in the world.

Here is an idea we got from a friend, but it has become a favorite of ours. Because of our schedule we find ourselves frequently eating out. When the wait-person brings our food, my husband will often say something like: "We're going to ask the Lord to bless our food; is there anything you'd like for us to ask Him to bless for you?"

The responses are almost always positive. From, "Ask Him to heal my wrist so I can carry these heavy trays," to one just the other day who said, "Just ask Him to bless my four children with good health." Besides our genuine interest in the one who is serving us, it may also give the Holy Spirit something new to work with in their life.

Please don't be misled by the term "banana bread" in the sub-title of the book. At first glance some may think, "Well, banana bread... this must be a women-only thing." Not so. Because the options are virtually infinite. Washing windshields in a supermarket parking lot, feeding expired parking meters, a car-care class for single women, handing out granola bars during morning rush hour at a busy intersection, free car washes, free pizza on dorm move-in days…the list is virtually endless. And with each event, a simple card that says, "Just showing God's love in a practical way," and the name and contact information for your church. Bridges.

Low-risk/high-grace; **you can *do* this.**

You'll want to get acquainted with Steve Sjogren's books. Some of them are classics, and they're filled with scores of suggestions. Try "Conspiracy of Kindness," or "101 Ways to Reach Your Community." Steve coined the phrase *"low-risk/high-grace"* which he has graciously allowed us to use here.

Chapter 4

Let's Be Scared Together

D oes it really work? To answer that question, let me ask another. Why are you doing it? If you are really wanting to serve others, and asking the Holy Spirit to touch and bless someone through you, then maybe it isn't a good idea to try to measure the responses of those you're serving.

We get impatient—we want to see "results" immediately. Maybe that's why Jesus told the story of the seed-sowing. Planting the seed may not be very dramatic, but it's essential for a harvest.

It usually takes numerous exposures to the Gospel before an unbeliever begins to see the light, and sees his need of a Savior. We cannot know where someone else is along this journey, but we don't need to. We are just asked to be faithful, to plant seed, to reach out, to help others, and to share God's love in a practical way. It generally takes time to build a bridge. We see the projects we're describing not so much as events, as they are pieces of a process, not so much as destinations as parts of a journey.

One of the medieval theologians discovered this many centuries ago, when he said, "Preach the Gospel wherever you can, and when necessary, use words."

We don't have a spiritual barometer that would measure what God is doing in human hearts as the result of our seed-sowing. But we've never been asked to be responsible for something that only He can do. He only asks us to be *faithful,* not bookkeepers. And when we are faithful, even a smile can have eternal consequences. We don't understand it, but He can do anything.

Our part is to prepare.

So let's say you have decided on a low-risk/high-grace project, maybe washing windshields in a super-market parking lot. You've talked it around quite a bit and you have a nice-size group that sees this as something they can do, maybe half a dozen. So you decide on the time and place.

Most events like this don't need to be long—an hour or two is enough, and it generally leaves your team with enough positive experiences to look forward to the next time.

So, how to begin. A friend of mine in the National Prayer Committee likes to say, "Until you know you're in a WAR, you'll never know what praying's for." That's probably a truism that's been passed down through generations of Christians doing offensive ministry.

And this is offensive warfare. The enemy is not going to cheer when he sees us out tangibly sharing God's love with someone who's lost. He'll create roadblocks and obstacles. That's why the weapon of prayer is so vital.

Prepare by prayer and claiming His promises. No matter how simple the adventure may be, *you dare not go alone,* but He has promised to be with us. Fact is, the prayer experience is so crucial we'll devote the entire next chapter to it.

Next step: You'll do better if your group members understand what to do and how to do it. So take a few minutes to brief the group before going out. Be sure each one understands what is expected. They'll be more comfortable when they get to the site. Take 10-15 minutes to go over the main details: where you'll be working, how to get there, who is in charge, where to go for more supplies, and any other details.

Steve Sjogren, in his book "Conspiracy of Kindness," says that it's expected that some will feel a little afraid at first, but he says, "That's OK, I'm scared too, let's go and be scared together."

It's obvious you'll need to take whatever supplies you'll be using. For a windshield-washing activity, for instance, you'll need good-quality cleaning supplies—wash-

"I'm scared too"

ing fluids, paper towels, squeegees, whatever. And of course, a good supply of cards that say, "We're just showing God's love in a practical way," with the name, address and contact information of your church on the reverse.

Once your team is out at the site and contacting people, they often realize that, as one person described it, "God shows up, and breaks down barriers, and often gives evidence that He is there."

One woman, when handed a hot drink at an intersection on her way home from work, took the glass, thanked the team-member, and then as she glanced down at the card he had handed her, she blinked in amazement. The card simply read, "Showing God's love in a practical way." As she thought about what she was reading, she realized that she was holding something tangible in her hand that had real meaning as a demonstration of God's love.

She later would tell the pastor—"The more I thought about it, the more I realized God was showing me His love, and I wept all the way home."

Our merciful God must enjoy being with His children, and even surprising them with His loving presence. Hosea quotes God as saying, "I drew them to me with cords of love and kindness. I picked them up and *held them to my cheek.* I took the yoke from their backs and bent down to them and fed them." (Hosea 11:4, Clear Word)

What a picture! The God of the universe, the Creator of heaven and earth is so deeply in love with His people that He picks us up and holds us to His cheek. He promises to go with us when we are out doing something in His name. He sends His angels to guard, to protect, and to strengthen.

David tells us that "the angel of the Lord guards and rescues those who reverence Him." (Psalm 34:7 TLB) Now, there's a promise we can claim!

And what about His incredible covenant promise from Psalm 121:5-8 (TLB):

"Jehovah Himself is caring for you! He is your defender. He protects you day and night. He keeps you from all evil, and preserves your life. He keeps his eye upon you as you come and go, and always guards you."

Sometimes the activities generate such spontaneous gratitude, or questions from those you serve, you can't wait to tell your other team members how you saw the God of heaven at work.

So after these team activities, be sure to provide a few minutes to de-brief and thank the Lord together for what He did. This will also be a good time to talk about what you could have done differently. Each experience can be a learning event, for greater effectiveness next time.

One group of men met at a Shoney's Big Boy Restaurant one evening following an outreach activity to share stories and de-brief. They were encouraged to hear how their simple ministries had touched some hearts.

But as they met around their table at the restaurant, they noticed that their waitress seemed especially distressed. One of the men finally asked her if she was OK.

"The dishwasher didn't come in tonight," she said, "so we have to clean and prepare our own tables, wash dishes, and still keep all the customers happy. It's impossible!"

The guys shared knowing glances, then sprang into action. One grabbed a tray and started clearing tables. Another went into the dishroom and started washing dishes; others found a broom or vacuum and started tidying up the dining room. When the manager walked into the dishroom he said, "I don't know if I can allow you to do this; it may be against company policy or something."

Before long, the place was clean, order was restored, and the waitresses were smiling—for the first time all evening. Even the manager had to admit that these guys were really special.

When they were asked why they were doing this, they'd just smile, and say, "We're just demonstrating God's love in a practical way." God's presence was there because His children were loving others in His name. Even the other customers enjoyed the little drama in the restaurant that evening.

These are simple things, but they leave a long-lasting reminder of your presence and good will, and most importantly, you have done something for Him, you've been working for Him—with Him—in Kingdom business on earth. Building bridges.

Chapter 5

Why I Love Bridges

You've met them, I know...people who just love to give things away. They're fun to be around because there is something about the act of giving that creates happy. For the *giver* as well as for the *givee* (if that's a word).

Our kids talk about people who have an attitude. Giving is an attitude.

Our neighbor, Donna, volunteers with a great organization called Meals on Wheels. She got started because another neighbor wanted to be helpful but wasn't sure how. So Donna signed up, and together they deliver food to shut-ins, and it has been a happy-making experience for both of them, as well as for those they serve.

Not long ago I ran into them in the library. They were looking for some specific books they were sure some of their geriatric home-bound clients would enjoy.

Another time I met Donna downtown and learned that she was shopping for a little stool with casters. She explained that she knew an elderly gentleman who couldn't walk around in his kitchen very well, but he could get around easily if he had a little "scooting chair." She found one, bought it and delivered it. Two happy people!

It seems that every time I see her, Donna's doing something for someone. We live in the same neighborhood, and she always knows, even though there are over a hundred families on our mountain, which ones have special needs—who is sick, who has just lost a loved one. And as a result of her beautiful "attitude," every time I see her she is beaming with joy, and has a new story to tell.

Few things give greater joy than giving. Are you a giver? Do you look for ways to give and people to give to? When we give, it broadens our horizons, it "enlarges our territory." Remember Jabez in the Old Testament? Jabez prayed that God would enlarge his territory, his life, his vision, his work, his abilities. God must have liked that prayer, because the Bible says that God blessed him when he made that request.

Jesus gave us a fascinating promise when He said, "Give and it will be given to you." (Luke 6:38) That means that when we begin what I call the cycle of sufficiency it opens the hands of God. When we give away some of even what we don't have enough of, God says He'll give it back, and more. Need happiness? Give some away. Need love? Give some away. Need time? Give some away. His promises never fail.

Maybe you saw the true story by Barbara Glanz that made the rounds on the internet not long ago. This is the story she tells:

"A few years ago I was hired by a large supermarket chain to lead a customer service program to build customer loyalty.

"During my speech, I said, 'Everyone can make a difference and create memories for your customers that will bring happiness and they will remember you.'

"I told them, 'Put your personal signature on the job...think about something you can do to make your customers feel special—a memory that will motivate them and make them want to come back.'

"About a month after I had spoken, I received a call from a 19-yr old [grocery] bagger. He proudly informed me that he was a Downs Syndrome individual and told me his story.

"'I liked what you talked about,' he said, 'but at first I didn't think I could do anything special for my customers. After all, I'm just a bagger.'

"'Then I had an idea,' Johnny said.

"I'm just a bagger"

"'Every night I'd come home and find a 'Thought for the Day.' If I couldn't find a saying I liked, I'd just think one up.'

"When Johnny had a good 'thought for the day,' his Dad helped him set it up on the computer and print multiple copies. "He cut out each quote, signed his name on the back, and took them to work the next day.

"'When I finished bagging someone's groceries,' he said, 'I'd put the 'Thought for the Day' in the bag, and say, 'Thanks for shopping with us.'

"It touched me that this man, with a job that most people wouldn't think was important, had made it important by creating personal memories for his customers.

"A month later the manager of that supermarket called me. 'You wouldn't believe what happened when I was making my rounds today,' he said. 'I found Johnny's line three times as long as anyone else's. It went clear down the frozen food aisle!'

"'We need more cashiers,' I said. 'Let's get more lines open.'

"As I tried to get people to change lanes, no one would move. 'It's

OK,' they'd say, 'we want to be in Johnny's line....We want his 'Thought for the Day.'"

"The store manager continued, 'It was a joy to watch Johnny delight his customers. It gave me a lump in my throat when one woman said, 'I used to shop at your store once a week, but now I come in every time I go by because I want to get Johnny's 'Thought for the Day.'

"A few months later the manager called me again, 'Johnny has transformed our store,' he said. 'Now when the Floral Department has an unused corsage, or some extra flowers, they find an elderly woman or a little girl, and pin it on them. Everyone is having a lot of fun creating memories.'

"A wonderful spirit of service spread throughout the entire store. All because Johnny chose to make a difference.

"'Our customers are talking about us,' the manager said. 'They're coming back and they're bringing their friends!'"

Johnny's idea wasn't so much innovative as it was loving. It came from his heart. It touched his peers and customers, and the story still touches us today. It's an attitude.

Great service comes from the heart, a heart willing to focus on someone in need...willing to develop an attitude of giving for those around us.

The late Gospel singer, Keith Green said, "It's so hard to see when my eyes are on *me*." (Emphasis supplied.)

If *you're* having a problem, help someone else solve *their* problem.

When we meet others with needs and we help them, God will help to meet our own needs. When we sow seeds of kindness, God brings a rich harvest.

When we do good things for others, we do good things for God. That's what Jesus taught. (Matthew 25:34-36) He didn't say, "I was lonely and you built a retirement home. I was sick and you worked to get me signed up on health insurance. I was in prison and you picketed the jail. I was thirsty and you gave me spiritual counsel."

No, He asks us to do simple things, without fanfare, no hoopla, no media coverage—just good people doing good things.

Ezekiel (34:26) describes this two-sided process: "I will make them a blessing, and there will be showers of blessings."

He actually goes so far as to say that He (God) will be "hallowed *in you* before their eyes." (v.25) When we help others, they see Someone more than us. Now that's pretty amazing, isn't it?

Visit a nursing home, or children's hospital. Visit a lonely neighbor. Call a friend, and give them a gift of courage.

You might say, "I don't have anything to give." Yes, you do. You can give a smile, you can bake someone a loaf of banana bread, or cookies. You can give someone a warm pie, a warm hug. You can hold a hand and say a prayer. You can write an encouraging note to someone who needs it. You can mow someone's lawn. Somebody needs what perhaps only you can give them.

"Lay your hand on the picture"

My husband was traveling in Japan and paging through a magazine written in Japanese—one he had not seen before. But he had extra time on the plane, so he was just looking with curiosity at the pictures and the layout.

He came across a very unusual advertisement. The Japanese man in the seat beside him asked him if he understood it. He admitted that he didn't. It was simply a gray, rather drab picture of a butterfly. But because the caption under the photo was in Japanese, Don couldn't read it.

The man beside him said, "Lay your hand on the picture." When he did, in just a few moments the warming of the special ink with which it was printed caused it to turn all the beautiful colors of a butterfly.

Who in your world needs a warm hand to help them blossom and come alive? Today.

There really is a new joy in our own hearts when we start every day by asking the Lord to lead us to someone we can bless. He will give us more joy than we ever thought possible. He'll pour out new blessings when we make the decision to be givers.

You may have read the amazing newspaper story about a set of twins who were just a few days old. One of them had been born with a heart condition and some of the medical staff feared that she might not live. A few days went by and the baby's health continued to deteriorate.

A hospital nurse asked if she could go against hospital policy and put the babies in the same incubator, together, rather than in individual incubators. It was a big ordeal, but finally the doctor consented to allow the twins to be placed side by side, just as they had been in their mother's womb.

Somehow, the healthy baby managed to reach over and put his arm around his little sick sister. Before long, and for no apparent reason, her heart began to stabilize and heal. Her blood pressure came up to normal. Her temperature soon followed suit. Little by little she got better, and today they are both strong, healthy children.

A newspaper got wind of the story and photographed the twins while still in the incubator, embraced in a hug. They ran the photo with the caption:

"The Rescuing Hug."

Who needs your hug? Who in your world needs a word of encouragement?

It doesn't take much time to reach out to someone. When we focus on being a blessing God will make sure that we are blessed. Look for opportunities to be a blesser.

It's an attitude. The still small voice of the Holy Spirit is prompting you to find someone you can help. It's a privilege to give, so be open to the voice.

We are never more like the heart of God than when we care for those who need His love. The only time in all the Scripture story that God is depicted as running is toward someone who didn't deserve it. (Luke 15:20)

There are people all around us He'd love to love through you and me today. And He will, if we're looking...if we have an attitude like His, the Great Giver, the Great Bridge Builder.

Chapter 6

You're a Perfect Candidate

If you could write the script, how many baptisms would you like to see in your local church next month? Next year? *If you could write the script*, would it include new people, neighbors, friends, by the score, shaking hands with the greeters at the door of your church every week?

If you could write the script, would you see hoards of people you've never met vying for space in the parking lot and coming early to church to make sure they can get a seat? *If you could write the script*, would you see the majority of your members active in witnessing? Every week?

Because I know your heart, I know you've answered Yes to every one of those questions. So, what stands between *Yes* and *reality*? If that's not what's happening in your church, do you know why?

OK, here's another question: Can we believe God's pledge that He will make His people "the head and not the tail"? (Deut. 28:13) And how about this promise: "Be strong and of good courage, and do it; do not fear nor be dismayed for the Lord God—my God—will be with you. He will not leave you nor forsake you, until you have finished all the work…" (IChron 28:20 NKJV)

You know the promises about "thousands in a day…" and others like it. If not now, when?

That leads me to ask, *What if God wrote the script*? How many folks would there be eagerly desiring to become members of your church family?

I believe those are all important questions and that we need to be absolutely, uncomfortably honest with our answers. Here is the issue as I see it: The project in which we are engaged is called spiritual warfare. Spiritual warfare demands supernatural resources…simple methods saturated with the Spirit of God. Unbeatable strategy. Unprecedented outcomes. Astonishing results.

Therefore…

Therefore you and I find ourselves in an enviable position: We are unquestionably perfect candidates for the extraordinary touch of God. He gives us an impossible assignment, then promises to live in us and make it possible.

Our friend, Rodney Griffin (Southern Gospel's Songwriter of the Year for the past nine years in a row) has set our predicament to music. He likens it to our standing on the shore of the Red Sea. It goes like this:

A Perfect Candidate

The situation looked so hopeless there for brother Moses,
As God's people all were stranded by the sea—
Pharaoh's army comin'—death would be for certain,
And escape was an impossibility.

As the chariots drew closer, Moses faced the water,
And he raised his hands above his head to pray.

Well if I had been there watchin' and seen old Pharaoh comin'
I'd say, "Moses, there's something I should say!

"Well, it seems that you would make a perfect candidate
For a touch from the mighty hand of God.
The storm that you are facing, the tempest that is raging,
Is what makes you uniquely qualified.

"For if the road were easy, your faith would not be needed,
And you'd never feel His wonder in your life.
It seems that you would make a perfect candidate
For a touch from the mighty hand of God."

Rodney Griffin

Our combined prayers might go something like this: "Lord, the situation we've been talking about looks hopeless. We've dreamed this dream for so long. The only thing that seems certain is more of the same. But Lord, I'm coming to You just as Moses did because all through Scripture You have shown me that You are the God of remarkable answers.

"You are the God who hears and You have a heaven full of blessings for Your people who will dare to ask and believe in Your mighty name. By Your grace and mercy, make me a perfect candidate for a touch from the mighty hand of God!

"I come to You as Martin Luther did, when he prayed, 'I am weak, I am needy, I am helpless, and I am unworthy, but I am Your child, and I come to You in the mighty Name of Jesus.'

"Nothing in my hands I bring, but I come to You as Jehoshaphat looked to You when he was in grave trouble—when his little kingdom of Judah was about to be devoured by three enormous, combined armies. You saved him and his little nation that day as the choir went out ahead of the soldiers to battle! He had nowhere else to go, and neither do I. What an assurance to know that You have been so faithful to Your children throughout the centuries. You have never deviated from the promises You have made to Your people.

"Lord, I need a touch from the mighty hand of God today. The storm that I am facing, the battle that is raging is what makes me uniquely qualified. My road will not be easy, but if it were, I wouldn't know how much I need You, and I would never want to miss Your wonder in my life. What a privilege to be a perfect candidate for a touch from the mighty hand of God!"

"So I praise Your name for the great and familiar miracle at the Red Sea. I thank You that I can come to You for renewed hope when I face my struggles. Even though that rescue took place back then, it was right here on planet earth where Your believing children were in desperate need.

"I praise Your name for what You did for people like George Mueller, Bill Bright, Reese Howells, James White, HMS Richards, Derek Morris, and so many others who have depended on Your intervening power. Our cause is central to Your plan. It is urgent. It is destined for success if it is driven by Your presence. So, Dear God, please do right now, today, for Your people what we cannot do for ourselves. We have given You our hearts; now we seek Yours. Amen."

Isn't it an amazing thing that we can talk to Him as we would to a friend whom we know really cares about us and is interested in what we're doing? He's the Creator of the universe, and we know His name!

You probably know about George Mueller, that great man of faith who lived during the 1800's in Bristol, England. One author has called Mueller the "Robber of the Cruel Streets," because, with no visible means of support, he took thousands of orphans off the streets and provided food, clothing, housing, and love for them. His audacity in what he asked God for may encourage you to "argue with God" as Mueller did.

Daily, faced with overwhelming needs and underwhelming resources, Mueller learned why King David was "delighted with God." He found that God was compassionate and trustworthy. He learned to "argue with God" as Abraham did. His arguments were strong because they were based on the promises of Scripture.

There were eleven points that Mueller often brought to God in prayer—reasons why he thought "the Lord would be pleased to answer." He was taking God's counsel through the prophet Isaiah very literally when he said, "Come now and let us reason together." Mueller's "arguments" are instructive to us today because we also are *perfect candidates* for a touch from the mighty hand of God, so we'll look at them in the next chapter.

Chapter 7

Mueller's "Arguments"

$180,000,000! That's right. In his lifetime George Mueller raised the equivalent in today's dollars of $180,000,000. The most amazing part of this story is that he never asked one person for a cent (or a pound).

Here is the story: In the early 1800's England had thousands of orphaned children running the streets, sleeping under bridges, eating out of garbage cans, with no social programs to rescue them. Historians say that there were more than 7,000 in England's prisons under the age of eight! Mueller and his wife, Mary, wanted to help them. But the couple had an even more pressing agenda. They wanted to give God an opportunity to demonstrate that He was faithful to supply the needs of those who ask Him.

In order to make the plan work, the Muellers covenanted together that they would ask only *God* for their needs and for the needs of the orphans. If someone asked him about his financial situation, Mueller always replied, "I only discuss those things with my "Heavenly Banker." He was consistent with that answer—even when resources were scarce —all his life.

Mueller explains in his own words his reasons…

> *"…for establishing an Orphan-House are: 1. That God may be glorified, should He be pleased to furnish me with the means, in its being seen that it is not a vain thing to trust in Him; and that thus the faith of His children may be strengthened."*

George and Mary began by remodeling their house to accommodate thirty young girls. They were housed, fed, clothed, educated, and loved. As the number of needy showing up at their doorstep increased they rented other facilities. In time they would build five massive stone buildings at Ashley Down in Bristol (which still stand—we've been there) that would house 2,000. Over the years that followed, the Muellers provided for a total of 10,024 youngsters, and never asked anyone for anything. Except God.

Mueller loved to tell about those times that were faith-stretchers. Although the children never missed a meal, there were times when they would be sitting at the table before a wagon-load of food would show up at the door.

For 30 years Mueller daily claimed the promise that God's blessings are "fresh every morning."

Mueller would sometimes come to his early-morning prayer times armed with a bucket of cold water. Some have said that he would even plunge his face into the shockingly cold water to revive himself if he got sleepy. He stayed there in his quiet place with God, "until I felt happy," he'd say. If he entered the room with a heavy heart or great needs, he didn't take them from that room. He gave them to God, and walked out with a light, happy heart.

Prayer became a passion. He could no more live without keeping his needs before his Father than he could live without breathing. When bills were paid and food was plentiful, Mueller prayed. When bills were mounting and food was scarce, Mueller prayed. When buildings or medical care for the children, or clothing, or food were needed, Mueller prayed. And God more than met his expectations. Mueller never tired of telling the stories of God's ample provision when there had been no other help in sight.

As the scope of Mueller's project increased and the complexity of providing for his growing family multiplied, he developed a list of reasons, or as he called them, *arguments*, which he presented to God as a rationale for why God should come to his rescue. You'll like these; they're strong. $180,000,000 strong!

1. He first reminded God that his work for the orphans was not his own work, it was God's idea, and done for His glory. Caring for the orphans was actually secondary—his primary reason for putting his faith on the line daily was to prove that God does answer prayer, yes, even in "our day," as he would say.

   If you are investing your life in ministry to others, you too can claim His promises which are "fresh every morning." He delights in demonstrating that He still keeps His Word, even in "our day."

   Remember: **"As for me, I am poor and needy, but the Lord is thinking about me right now. You are my help and my savior. Do not delay, O my God." (Ps 40:16, 17 NLT)**

2. His second argument was very specific: for the care of the orphans. Here was a group of very needy youngsters and He believed God cared about them.

   All throughout Scripture God's heart is very clear...He has a special love for the orphans, widows, and others who are disadvantaged. Are you at a disadvantage? Or are you reaching out to help those who are? Mueller thanked God for

*being a God of kindness and compassion, and for caring for
those in need. Are there disadvantaged folks in your community you could help? God loves to do that through His people.
Talk to Him about it.*

Remember, **"He relieves the fatherless and widow."
(Psalm 146:9)**

3. Mueller repeatedly told God that he had accepted the children *in
Christ's name* and that in these children Jesus was actually being
received, clothed, fed, and cared for. He told God he thought He
would be pleased to remember that.

    *Maybe you don't need to take orphaned children into your
    home—or maybe you could—but are there needy families...
    emotionally needy, spiritually needy, love-deprived, margin-
    alized, unemployed...to whom you could be an extension of
    God's loving hand?*

    Remember: **"Assuredly, I say to you, inasmuch as you
    did it to one of the least of these My brethren, <u>you did it
    to Me</u>." (Matthew 25:40)**

4. Mr. Mueller realized that the faith of many of God's people had
been strengthened by the answers to prayer for the orphans
under his care. He told God that if He were to withhold "means"
for the future, those who were weaker in their faith would be
affected measurably by that. But if God continued to pour out
His lavish answers, their faith would grow even stronger. He
knew how the community felt about his work.

    *The faith of others is often enhanced by our acts of faith.
    Even during WWII, the five large buildings that Mueller built
    were considered "holy ground."*

Instead of running to an underground bomb shelter during air raids, the citizens of Bristol would often go to one of Mueller's buildings. They knew they'd be safer there. When God does something big, the influence cannot be contained.

Remember: **"Call upon Me in the day of trouble; I will deliver you and you shall glorify Me." (Ps 50:15RSV)**

5. Mueller argued with God as he reminded Him that his enemies would be looking for reasons to doubt and ridicule. They were always ready to cast doubts and criticism not only on George Mueller, but on Mueller's God.

    In the spiritual battles we face, our very real spiritual enemy looks for someone who will laugh at your faith, who will tell you that you're being childish, naïve, too simple in your faith when you believe God's Word for big things. Mueller told God, "These people are expecting and hoping that this great work will come to nothing."

    Remember, **"In Your unfailing love, silence my enemies...for I am Your servant." (Ps 143:12)**

6. Mueller told God that because he had discovered how true He is to His promises, others too were learning how to trust Him with their needs. He could also see those around him who were relying on their "alliance with the world" in their work for God. He had a burning desire to teach and demonstrate that the divine arm is always greater than the "arm of flesh."

    Hudson Taylor, one of the scores of missionaries supported regularly by Mueller, once said, "God's work, done in God's way, will never lack for God's resources." Taylor learned that over and over in his work in the Inland China Mission, and has left his own legacy of a powerful life of faith.

Remember, **"With him is only the arm of flesh, but with us is the Lord our God to help us and to fight our battles." (II Chron. 32:8)**

7. His next argument was humbling and personal. He told the Lord, "Remember that I'm your child, and I cannot provide for these urgent needs." Then he pleaded with God not to "allow this burden to lie upon me long without sending help." He asked God to pity him because he was His helpless child.

   We are never stronger than when we sense our helplessness.

   Remember, **"...I am poor and needy; come quickly to me, O God. You are my help and my deliverer..." (Ps 70:5)**

8. Then Mueller asked God to remember all of his co-workers—his staff at the church where he was pastor (for 66 years!), and at the orphan homes. There were teachers, nurses, culinary helpers, housekeepers, and others. It required a large number of adults to care for the children as well as the hundreds of thousands of pounds he gave away to support other teachers, other schools, and other missionaries.

   Mueller describes even the lean years very positively. He was always "delighted with God," even when he could see no outward signs of God's answers. He would say that many probably thought it must have been difficult for him during those testing times, but his faith grew stronger with every dire test. Even so, those around you look to you for courage and confidence. When Mueller died, the entire city of Bristol shut down for his funeral because his life had blessed so many.

*Remember, **"I will offer you the sacrifice of thanksgiving, and will call upon the name of the Lord. I will pay my vows to the Lord now in the presence of all His people."** (Ps. 116:17, 18)*

9. Mr Mueller often thanked God for what He had done to bring spiritual instruction and a right environment to thousands of children and young people. Before the orphan homes were opened, many children were forced to sleep on the streets, or in jails or in the mental "asylums" because there was nowhere for them to go. Crimes were common because the hungry children robbed for food and warm clothing. He asked the Lord to remember that he would have to dismiss these precious little ones from under their "scriptural instruction" to their former companions on the streets.

What is God's dream for your ministry? I don't mean some time in the dim, distant future. I mean tomorrow. Who is there in your sphere of influence who may not feel a touch of love unless you touch them? How does God want you to change your world in the next twenty-four hours? The next ten years? Whatever your history, whatever your age, I have no question that your most effective days are just ahead.

*Remember: **"If you keep yourself pure, you will be a utensil God can use for His purpose. Your life will be clean, and you will be ready for the Master to use you for every good work."** (II Tim 2:21 NLT)*

10. There were skeptics in his community who were amazed when the work began, but who were convinced that it would never last. They didn't believe Mueller would be faithful in prayer and trust

only God. They weren't sure how long God would continue to lavish His answers on this undertaking. Mueller prayed, "Lord, show that those were mistaken who said that *at first* supplies might be expected, while the thing is new, but not afterward."

More than once, there would be an early morning knock at the door of one of the orphan homes. It might be a donation of food or money, with the explanation, "I just couldn't sleep all night...I was concerned about the needs of the children." The children never missed a meal and every bill was paid on time for half a century. Why do these often-repeated stories still have the power to inspire us with new courage? Because this is a God-thing, and God is honored as His children recount and remember what He has done in the past.

Remember: **"May Your unfailing love come to me, O Lord...then I will answer the one who taunts me, for I trust in Your Word." (Ps 119:41,42 NIV)**

11. Mueller's last "argument" was a very human one, yet still filled with faith. He told God, "You have blessed me so immeasurably and now if You were to withhold help, how would I ever understand the remarkable answers I have already received so far, and on a daily basis, for this work."

God provides direction for His people by providing—and by withholding—His resources. Our role is to present our needs, look for the indications of His providence, and then move with dispatch as He opens the way. The past generates faith for the future.

My friend, Charles Bradford, a retired church administrator, said he learned that powerful truth as a young pastor when he overheard two of his members talking about claiming Scripture promises. As he approached them, he heard one say to the other, "Hold Him to it, sister, hold Him to it."

*Remember: "...**Being confident of this, that he who began a good work in you will carry it on to completion until the day of Christ Jesus." (Phil 1:6 NIV)***

If you were to visit Ashley Down, in Bristol, England, today, you would find five huge stone buildings that still stand as a silent monument to the consistent power of the God who loves to answer prayer. These well-built, attractive buildings are now being used by a local college, and as luxury housing, although they were built more than a century and a half ago. God provided lavishly because of one man's faith, and today He is still looking for those who will take Him at His Word. I'll bet that includes you.

Chapter 8

The Safest Place to Be

It can seem a little daunting, especially when you think about all the possibilities, all the creative methods there are by which we can share God's love in practical ways. Where to start? Some will appeal to you more than others—we all have different gifts, different interests, different abilities.

You've heard this before, but it's no less important because it's familiar: *Spend time with God—talking to Him about His people, before you ever spend time with people—speaking to them, or doing anything for them—for the Kingdom.*

Here's an idea: Get together with one or two friends and pray. Better yet, prayerwalk, or prayerdrive the neighborhoods in your area. Pray for the businesses you pass, for the students and teachers in the schools you pass, for the customers in the bars you pass, for the families in the homes you pass.

Drive by the jails and pray. Drive by the government buildings and pray. Drive by the adult book stores and pray. Drive by the hospital and pray.

Amazing results can come from something as simple as that. Anyone—even the timid—can go prayerwalking, or prayerdriving, because it likely won't involve contact with anyone outside your little group. But the prayers can have eternal consequences—because of Who is listening.

If you're walking, keep the group small, two or three. Dress for walking, and don't carry a Bible, just get some physical and spiritual exercise. One person can pray aloud, while the others pray silently. Claim Scripture promises from memory, and ask God to give you His loving heart of compassion for His people in your community.

We hear the question, "Why not just stay at home and pray?" And you can do that. But when you're out in someone else's neighborhood you see their situation, and it's easier to really care for someone if you go where they are.

Jesus modeled that for us. One of the first steps in ministry is to go where people are. Christ mingled with people. He went where they were so he could get acquainted with them, then He met their needs. Only then did He say, "Follow Me."

It may give you insight into another's world. In fact, some have called prayerwalking "praying on-site with insight." You see what they're facing.

It's intentional, and it focuses on the specific neighborhood, homes, people, businesses, and schools you encounter.

The results may be dramatic and immediate. Or more likely, they may be neither of those. No matter; hearts are opened by prayer, and doors are often opened for God's healing touch. Prayerwalking is a stimulating way to stretch your prayers in new directions.

When Don and I moved from Maryland to the west coast of Florida, we were delighted with the "retirement atmosphere" in our neighborhood. It was almost like everyone was on vacation. We were both still working part-time, but the new schedule gave us some time to get acquainted.

In our neighborhood in Punta Gorda—all across Florida, actually—the terrain is *flat* (in fact, someone told us that the highest point in Florida is an overpass), so we could ride bicycles or walk, and we tried to establish a routine of walking every morning.

We started praying for our neighbors, every day by name, and before long, we began to see hearts and doors opening. We were invited to their events, and into their homes, and they came to ours.

One afternoon, as I rode my bike past Jack & Penny's home, just around the corner from us, Jack was out in his yard, so I stopped to visit. He looked a little worried, so I asked him how he was doing. He told me that the day before he had been diagnosed with leukemia, and they weren't sure what might lie ahead. Penny was understandably troubled, too.

"Jack, would it be OK if I pray for you right here?" I asked.

"Sure, Ruthie, go ahead," he responded. So I prayed for Jack and Penny, for peace, for hope, for direction, for healing. Jack was a retired executive from a large pharmaceutical company in Michigan. They had lived in Punta Gorda for more than ten years and everybody in the neighborhood loved them. Jack was especially close to his golfing buddies.

We visited with Jack and Penny often after that. Because I was the only nurse in the neighborhood, I became the liaison between them and the doctors and the neighbors.

Penny wanted it that way. She wanted me to be part of the decisions and to pass on news to their friends. So as I contacted the neighbors, they always wanted to know about Jack's condition, and to have their greetings carried back to him.

We invited Jack's friends and other neighbors to pray for him. Most of them attended one of the area churches, if irregularly, somewhere in the community, and were pleased to be part of Jack's prayer support.

As the disease progressed, Jack had some difficult and dark days, but on one occasion when he came home from the hospital, the neighbors wanted to celebrate. We had a big "Jack is Back!" party. Jack's neighbor across the street, a retired vice-president from Ford Motor Company and his wife, wanted to have it in their home, and they put up a huge banner that said, "JACK IS BACK!" It was a wonderful evening.

As the party drew to a close, my husband suggested that we gather for a prayer of thanksgiving. We had been praying individually, and now we gathered in a circle to pray together, thanking God for Jack and for keeping him in His care. Don's prayer was a special moment in the evening, and drew us all a little closer.

We saw Jack and Penny often over the next months, and finally, as we could see the end drawing nearer, we prayed especially for God's sustaining presence. Jack told me, just before he died, that he had a new understanding and a new relationship with God through all of this. "I've attended church most of my life, but I really never knew God, until now." He had peace to the end.

"Jack is Back!"

We believe those relationships with all our neighbors were possible because we prayed for them daily by name—and still do—as we walked or rode our bikes by their homes. It begins with prayer.

Prayerwalking has three different approaches or levels. First, it's just walking down the sidewalk, praying for others, taking cues from whatever or whoever we see, and asking the Lord to guide our prayers and to open the hearts of those for whom we're praying. You probably won't actually make contact with them at this time, but you're praying and taking them before the throne of the universe.

There is a second type of prayerwalking, involving some contact with those for whom you're praying. Maybe you see someone in their yard and have an opportunity to visit and introduce yourself; you might tell them that you're just out walking and praying. You could ask them if they have any special prayer needs so you can be specific in your prayers.

Some teams prefer this method, and even knock on doors, asking for prayer requests. Almost without exception they are met with a positive response. It takes a little more courage, but if you've prayed about it first, you'll see how God does go before You and prepares the way, as He has promised. It's a wonderful way to make new friends.

The third level of ministry in prayerwalking is to be alert for someone you can lead to Christ, as the occasion presents itself. This doesn't happen as often, but it can make obvious that this casual walk is really Kingdom business.

One Sabbath morning a friend and I were in New York and we were out prayerwalking in Harlem. We noticed a man standing in front of his apartment building, so we approached him and asked if there was anything he would like for us to pray about for him. After we had prayed for his wife and daughter as he had requested, I sensed that he had some other needs.

"Do you know this God we've just been talking to?" I asked.

"No. I really don't, but I appreciated your prayers for my family," he responded.

He seemed open to our conversation, so I continued, "He created you, and loves you, and that's why we're here."

Then I said, "God really loves you and wants you to be in heaven, but if He should ask you why He should let you in, how would you answer?"

"Well, I don't suppose I have any reason I could give Him. I've tried to do my best, but I can't say I deserve heaven," he said.

"I don't deserve to be there, either, sir," I said.

He looked at me with big eyes, and I could see that he was ready for what I was explaining.

"No one could ever make it to heaven if Someone hadn't made sure there was a way," I said. I told him that Jesus' death was what was necessary to take care of the sins of the world—his and mine included.

"This is a gift, and there is no way we can be good enough to earn it. But we do have to choose to accept it, and to ask Him to forgive us and to come in and take charge in our lives," I explained.

"Is there any reason why *you* wouldn't want to accept this free Gift?" I asked.

"No," he said, thoughtfully, "I need that Gift."

"Then we need to pray again, don't we?" I asked.

He repeated the sinner's prayer after me, and I am convinced he meant it. We talked briefly about his new family—the family of God. Then he shook my hand enthusiastically, and thanked me for stopping by his home.

Prayerwalking is warfare

We invited him to come to the church, and he said he'd be there. He was beaming as we walked away, and we were thrilled to have watched the Holy Spirit transacting His great business of salvation.

Prayerwalking is warfare. It is contending with evil. We are literally stepping out from a defensive, fortress mentality and coming physically near to the people whom we know Jesus died to save. Remember, He "is not willing that *any* should perish." (2 Peter 3:9)

That's why prayerwalking can be so powerful—you are teaming up with the God of the armies of heaven to do the work He has asked you to do...love His children. And when you are working with Him, nothing is impossible.

Scary? Sure, for some. But it's ok to be scared for the right reason.

Have you ever put yourself in the story in Matthew 14, when Jesus approaches the disciples on that stormy night, *walking on the water*? Why do you suppose He put that story in Scripture? Could He have a special message of encouragement for us timid ones?

Could He have a great plan and purpose for your life that you haven't even imagined yet? Could your best, most productive days be just ahead?

There is a fascinating statement in Daniel which says that those who know Him intimately will be changed. (Daniel 11:32 ASV) He has promised to make you strong and able to do bold and daring things—not for yourself, but for Him.

My husband and I were enjoying a gospel concert in Pigeon Forge, Tennessee, last fall when we heard a song for the first time that immediately appealed to us both. The strength and truth of the words of the song are captivating and deep.

Here's the song—read the words thoughtfully. It has the informality of a southern gospel song, but it also has a profound depth. It may give you just the encouragement you're looking for:

Get Out of the Boat

Peter started walkin' out on the water one dark and stormy day,
But Peter started sinkin' when Peter started thinkin' about how he
    was afraid.
Eleven disciples watched, as Jesus reached His hand to help.
They saw it, it's true, but they never knew, how walking on the
    water felt.

Chorus:

Get out of the boat, start walking on the sea.

'Cause out of the boat is the *safest place to be.*

When you're walking toward the Master, He will keep you afloat.

Don't be afraid of the wind or the waves.

Come on, come on, come on—get out of the boat.

Think of John and Matthew, Thomas and Andrew—all safe inside
the ship.

Maybe they were hoping that they could keep on floating,

But oh, the thrill they missed.

I know it can be scary, when you trust the Lord that way,

*But if you never get wet, or get in over your head—you really can't
call it faith.*

Get out of the boat, start walking on the sea.

'Cause out of the boat is the *safest place to be.*

When you're walking toward the Master, He will keep you afloat.

Don't be afraid of the wind or the waves,

Come on, come on, come on—get out of the boat.

Joel Lindsay & Sue C. Smith

I believe that's His call to your heart and mine. Today.

Christian author, Dr. Henry Blackaby, spent a day with us at the
National Prayer Committee a couple of years ago when we met in Palm
Springs, California. After he had shared some powerful teaching from
God's Word, he said, "Now I want you to get away, by yourself, and pro-
cess this. What is God saying to you, personally through these insights?
What meaning does this have for you individually, and for His work?"

So, I have an assignment for you as you have been reading: Reflect back on the issues we have talked about in the "Bridges 101" book. Ask God earnestly, "What is the message You have for me personally? What are the next steps You want me to take? What plan and purpose do You have for me? What new dreams do You have for me to dream?

"You have said that just as surely as there is a place for me in heaven, there is a place for me right here on earth where I am to serve You and others.

"Please show me the next steps, and give me a willing, eager heart to invest my life in the lives of others.

"Then someday in Your kingdom, I believe you'll show me the faces of the people who are there because You and I had a wonderful adventure together building bridges, right here in Your world. Amen."

Chapter 9

The Singing, Dancing, Painter

He was standing outside Michelle's Beauty Shop, and as I approached to get my hair cut that morning, he held the door open for me. "Be careful, young lady," he said (I really liked that part), "I'm painting the trim, and this black paint is wet." I thanked him and walked in.

But I have to tell you that I was a little surprised to meet him. It's not every day that you meet *a singing, dancing, painter.* He had a headset on and an iPod in his pocket. He enthusiastically sang along with Bob Dylan, and his feet moved in happy rhythm as he painted. Some spectacle! This was a first for me.

As I walked into the shop, everyone seemed to be talking about the musical painter, so I asked, "Who is he?" They all seemed to know him.

"He's Hugh Burke," they told me, "and he sings around town, like for the United Community Bank's annual concert."

I thought the Lord gave me a great idea. Why not invite him to come to our church to sing?

So after Michelle finished with my hair, I went outside looking for

Mr. Burke. By this time he was around on the other side of the building, painting the trim on the offices there. I walked over to him and motioned that I wanted to talk to him. He took off the headset and climbed down the ladder.

I explained to him that we attend church in Blairsville, just fifteen minutes away, and asked him if he would come and sing for us some Saturday morning.

"I'd like to, but I just can't," he said. "I don't think I could sing in a church right now. I'm not 'there' with the Lord," he reflected.

"Don't you think God would like to hear you sing?" I asked. He smiled, and thought about that a moment.

"Hey, I've just written a book by that title," I told him. "It's called, 'God Wants to Hear You Sing.' Would you like to read it? It's about the importance of praising God, even though we may be walking through a difficult time."

"Sure, if you wrote a book, I'll read it," he promised. He told me where he'd be working the next day so I could deliver it.

The next day I returned with a copy of my book, and he seemed genuinely glad to get it. "I'll tell you what I'll do," he said. He had obviously been thinking about my invitation. "Tell you what—I'll sing in your church if you'll sing with me. Let's do a duet."

Well, I saw that as great progress because the day before he had told me he wouldn't come at all. So I said, "Sure, I'll be glad to sing a duet with you." Now, I'm not a great singer, but I'll do almost *anything* to get someone to come to church with me.

A couple of days later Don and I were driving in town, and I saw him working at another shopping center on the east side of Hiawassee. So we stopped and I introduced Don and Hugh. We visited a few minutes and then Hugh said, "Ruthie, I can't come to your church *this* Saturday, but I could sing with you there *next* week."

As we drove away we found ourselves thanking the Lord that He had been working on Hugh's heart, softening it. We decided on a time to practice and invited him to lunch the next day. We'd have a sandwich and then work on our song.

It was interesting to sing with him. He knew all the songs, but he was extremely selective.

"Do you know 'All To Jesus I Surrender?'" he asked. "Sure, do you want to sing that song?" I asked.

"No, not *that* song," he quickly replied.

He finally chose "Great Is Thy Faithfulness." Perhaps not an ideal song for a duet, but that's OK. That was his choice, so we started singing.

The first verse went pretty well and then I said, "Hugh, you have a great tenor voice, and I think we'd all like to hear you sing the second stanza alone."

So he began, "*Summer and winter, and springtime and harvest, Sun, moon and stars in their courses above, Join with all nature in manifold witness—To Thy great faithfulness, mercy and love.*"

I could see that he was struggling with his emotions as he sang. Tears were in his eyes, his voice broke, and he finally just stopped. "I can't do that!" he said, quietly. "I don't want to cry at your church."

"Let me tell you something that just happened a couple of weeks ago in a little church where my husband and I were visiting," I told him.

"Our friend, Sarah, was leading the morning Bible study time, but before she got started, she told us why she was so tired and so unable to concentrate.

"'The girlfriend of my son, Ted, called us in the wee hours this morning to tell us that our 18-yr. old son, an alcoholic, was 'out of control.' 'Come and do something,' she begged.

"'So my husband, Zack, and I went over and tried to reason with him. We tried everything, but he only mocked us. He threw our sins up before us—alcohol, drugs, immorality—he knew them all.

"'Yes, Ted, you're right,' I told him, 'but Zack and I have given that all to God and asked Him to change us, and he has; our lives have changed. We're forgiven, and you can be too.'

"'We couldn't seem to penetrate his alcohol-numbed mind. It was getting late and I knew we had to leave for church; I was leading out in the lesson this morning, but how could I do that?

"'Finally, in desperation, I asked my mother to come stay with Ted, and Zack and I drove to church. So here we are, but I can't think of anything but Ted,' Sarah explained. By now she was weeping as she bravely shared her heart with us.

What church is all about

"A lady from the class walked up to stand beside Sarah, and hugged her. 'Let's show Sarah and Zack what church is all about,' she said to the group. 'Help me make a big circle, right here at the front. Let's agree in prayer and ask God to do His work in Ted's life today.' So we prayed together, and all of us were weeping as we lifted her precious son before the Lord.

"Finally, my husband said, 'Lord, please do something specific in Ted's life this morning. If he's awake, help him to sleep. If he's asleep, wake him up, but touch his heart with Your deep message of love.'

"A new peace settled over the group, and we thanked the Lord for hearing our prayers. Sarah beamed with a new serenity, and went on to finish the lesson.

"Later, as they were driving home from church, she phoned her mother and asked about Ted. 'The strangest thing happened this morning,' her mom reported.

"'Ted was sound asleep, but he woke up, bolted out of bed, and ran for the bathroom—deathly sick, and vomited repeatedly. Finally he came out of his room, and said to me, 'Grandma, I can't drink anymore. It'll kill me.'"

"'What time was that?' Sarah asked her mother.

"'I don't know, 10:00, or maybe 10:15.' 'That's right when we were praying!' Sarah replied."

As I shared that story with Hugh, he smiled. "It's OK to be real in church," I said. "God is there, and His Spirit touches hearts. When we see Him work, we can't help but rejoice."

So Hugh came to our church the next week. We have a praise time each Sabbath morning when a hand mic is brought to anyone who would like to share a special praise—usually something that has happened just that week.

I was a little surprised when Hugh raised his hand to speak, and he didn't stay seated as everyone else had. He stood to his feet, and exclaimed happily, "I just praise the Lord that I am here! I thank God for the way He allows paths to cross."

Just before we sang our duet, Hugh again wanted to speak. "Last night my wife and I were out driving in our little convertible, and as we looked up and saw the beautiful sky, again we were aware of God's goodness and mercy. Ruthie and I want to sing now about His faithfulness," he said.

But our accompanist had to play the introduction through a couple of times, while Hugh got his emotions under control. The congregation, too, was touched to sense the reality of God's presence there in our midst—as He promised.

After the song, Pastor David stood up to speak. "We could go home right now," he said. "We've been deeply blessed. But, Hugh, the next time you come to sing, we're going to put a box of tissues under every seat."

Let me tell you what God taught me from Hugh Burke:

1. God can use the most unlikely circumstances if we are looking for ways to be useful.

2. God never gives up on us; He'll even chase us up ladders.

3. God has a wonderful sense of humor.

We keep in touch with Hugh. He's a friend whom God loves enough to orchestrate strange meetings, and to be sure that paths supernaturally cross.

So keep watching. You may find a Hugh at the grocery store, at the gas station, at the post office, next door. Or even up a ladder somewhere. And who knows, he may even be singing, dancing, and painting.

Chapter 10

Gas Pumps

My husband was having his hair cut the other day and a couple of people in the shop were talking about a traffic tie-up they had seen in town the afternoon before.

One lady said she at first thought it was a bad accident, but as she drove by she discovered it was a gas station with a ridiculously low price...50 cents less per gallon than anywhere else in town! Cars were lined up clear down the street.

Don's barber chimed in, "Yes, it was some people from the Seventh-day Adventist Church, just doing something nice for our community to 'show God's love in a practical way.' At least that's what the card said that they gave me. It was pretty nice, really."

The decision to do a "gas buy-down"—not an original idea with us, by the way—grew out of a desire to do something for our community that could be helpful to a lot of people, and from some intense prayer sessions where we pled with the Lord to show us how we could tangibly love our neighbors on His behalf. We'd claim promises like, "I Myself will go with you and give you success." (Exodus 33:14 TLB)

With gasoline prices at an all-time high, many drivers are really feeling the crunch, and would welcome any news of a place to buy gasoline at a lower price—even if for a short time.

We contacted a couple of the major gasoline companies and discovered that this might not be as easy as we thought. The request had to go through all kinds of corporate red tape and be approved by everyone in the building. It took two weeks before we finally decided that we might have to pursue a different strategy.

So we found a "mom and pop" station and approached them. Our proposal was that for two hours—4:00 to 6:00—on the evening selected, they would sell gas for $2.75 rather than the posted $3.25. We would have our church crew on site to welcome the folks, wash windshields, and hand out cards with the name and address of our church and our website. Then when it was all over we'd write the station a check for the difference.

We did the math and came up with the estimate that each of the four pumps at the station would handle a dozen cars per hour. In two hours that would mean about a hundred cars. If they averaged 10 gallons per car, that would be 1,000 gallons. If we paid the station the difference of 50 cents/gallon the total cost to us would be about $500. Sounded like a good idea.

Our calculations were pretty close. Actually, we sold gas to just about exactly a hundred cars, for a total of 952 gallons. Total cost, including supplies: almost exactly $500. But that's not the most important thing that happened.

We did a bit of inexpensive advertising for the event in two ways. First, we visited maybe twelve or fifteen businesses in our town. (Remember, this is Hiawassee, Georgia, not Atlanta.) Here we handed out small 4X6 cards that said, "Gasoline (regular unleaded) - $2.75/gallon." We gave the location and time of the special sale. Often as we would walk out of the store or bank or post office, folks had gathered around the little pile of cards and it was already creating quite a stir. I mean, in our little town, this was a big deal.

We also contacted Mike Savage, manager of our local radio station. When we told him about the plan he was pleased to run the item as a PSA—Public Service Announcement—during the day of the buy-down, at no cost.

It's hard to say which was more effective. Some of the customers would say, "My neighbor heard about it on the radio and called me." Apparently there are several grapevines that work well in our town.

One lady where we were leaving cards said, "Who is doing this, and why?" "It's the Blairsville Seventh-day Adventist Church," we answered, "and we're doing it to show God's love in a practical way. We wanted to do something for our community, and decided that right now some relief from the gas prices might help."

"God bless you!" she replied. "And thank you." Everywhere we went with the cards announcing the event, we were met with appreciation and excitement.

We chose a gas station that had a good traffic flow because of the long lines we anticipated. But as we headed for the station about 15 minutes before the announced time, we wondered if anyone really would show up. We were not disappointed. By the time we arrived, there were long lines down the street in both directions. One line reached clear to the driveway of the next service station.

When we were making the arrangements, the manager of the station we were using warned us. "I've seen people have to wait in long gas lines, and it can get pretty ugly. I mean, I've seen fights...bloody knuckles...people don't like to wait to buy gas." Boy, was he in for a surprise.

There was a pleasant banter and excitement—it felt almost like a party. It gave our customers a good feeling to be able to "beat the system" even if it was only for one tank of gas. We walked up and down the lines of cars, welcoming them to the event, handing out granola bars and our little welcome cards that explained who was doing the project and why.

The card said:

"Just showing God's love in a practical way," with a little smiley sticker on one side. The other side gave the name of our church, the address, website, and the cell phone number of our pastor. (You might want to clear this with your pastor!)

Some of the conversations with the customers were short, some longer, but it was a great opportunity to get acquainted, us with them and they with us. One of the pumps was slower than the others, and when someone pulled up to that pump we'd say, "We put just special people here because it gives us longer to chat with them."

"And did I mention smiling?"

Our pastor, David Wright, Ron and Jelaine Westfall, and my husband and I were the team. We spent two wonderful hours washing windshields, smiling, directing traffic, smiling, greeting and handing out the snacks and connection cards. Oh, and did I mention smiling? And we answered a lot of questions. Not theological questions, you understand. Friendship questions. It was orderly and it was fun.

There were some particularly moving moments on the parking apron of the station. For instance, as the 6:00 deadline drew near I approached one car and spoke to the lady who was driving. As we spoke I noted her husband beside her. He didn't look as though he felt well and he had a patch over one eye.

As we visited I learned that Bruce, a man I judged to be about 50, had recently suffered a serious stroke. As a result, he was left with double vision and the doctors were saying it was doubtful whether he might ever be able to work again.

They had just come from the specialist's office in Atlanta where Bruce had had his second MRI. The physicians were puzzled about the cause of the stroke, and were cautious about giving him any good news of what he might expect in the future.

Seeing their obvious concern, I leaned close and asked, "Would it be ok if I would pray for you right here?" "I'd appreciate that," Bruce replied.

And so we prayed together, asking for God's special intervention and guidance for the future, and Bruce was beaming as he thanked me. God provides "out of the box" opportunities, even standing in a gas line at a service station.

Someone asked me if we were expecting that these gasoline-buyers would keep their cards and come to church the next week. No. Not necessarily. At least, not many. (Although at least one young man asked for specific directions to our church.) We were out there as "seed fling-ers." This was not as much an *event* as it was a *part of a process*: provid-ing the Holy Spirit with another opportunity to reach someone's heart with the message that they are loved by God.

We had the marvelous opportunity of meeting and talking with a large number of new people we probably would never have met in any other way.

We were pleased when people would ask where our church was and time of services, but our primary goal was to show God's love in a practical way.

One lady, a clerk at McDonald's, when we handed her an announce-ment card the day before, exclaimed, "Great! Now I can go fill my tank. I haven't bought more than $20 at any one time since the prices have gone up. That's my limit." Hers was one of the first cars in line, and she thanked us over and over.

A reporter came from our local newspaper and asked questions of some of those in line as well as those of us who were serving. He took pictures of some of the customers pumping gas and of our crew washing windshields.

He also got a positive report about our church group from the folks who operate the station. A few days later the project made the front page of the paper (actually, the front page of both of our local papers) —color picture and all.

Under the headline, "God's love and gasoline," here are some of the things they said about our project: "Big D assistant manager Shonna Challis said at first the customers thought the reduced gas price was a store promotion, only to find out there was a church sponsoring it. 'They did something that was remarkable. The customers really appreciated it,' she said. 'They know that every-body is struggling right now...They [did] it to help us out.'"

"They did it to help us out"

The next morning as I drove by I noticed the price of gas at that station had gone back to "normal," and then, up another 8 cents.

Our learnings:

Probably the most important thing we learned is that this is an amazingly simple but highly visible way for our church to do something positive for the community. It gave us a chance to do something for others—something they needed and were glad to get. It positioned our church as people who are not exclusive, but willing to be of help to others in the community...in practical ways. And it created a climate for conversation and a pleasant meeting place. (By the way, you could lower your cost of doing the project by having the sale for only *one* hour, or by discounting the gas less than 50 cents.)

Here are a few practical tips to remember when you plan this kind of outreach:

1. Be sure to pray about each step—in contacting the right station manager, and in planning for the event...the time, the place, the price, the team. It's not just selling gas; it becomes a God-thing. My husband said he hadn't had this many hugs since the last time he performed a wedding.

2. Get a small group of people together to help who enjoy meeting and helping others. And smiling.

3. Have enough connection cards ready. Be sure they're attractive and include all the necessary information.

4. You'll need squeegees, buckets of water, and paper towels.

5. The snacks are optional. We decided to try it—and they were well received.

6. We met just before going to the station—to decide each person's responsibilities and to pray together. This is a vital step. When God is present He will often minister in unexpected ways. These are people who are special to Him.

7. Meet again right afterward to debrief. What could be changed for another time? What were the benefits? How could it be improved? This is really helpful because it gives the group a time to thank the Lord for what He did, and to stop and recount the joys of working for Him in this simple way.

The consensus of the group was, "This was great. Let's do it again. The obvious gratitude was worth it all."

We're already planning the next one.

Chapter 11

Bridge Builders

You've noticed that bridges come in all shapes, colors, and sizes. They're made of different materials. Some are covered, some are short, some are long, one-lane, two-lane, four-lane, but they serve a common purpose: they all connect things.

The people who *build* bridges also come in all shapes, sizes, and colors.

Let me tell you about some delightful bridge builders. One, in our little church here in north Georgia, is Jim.

If you had met Jim a couple of years ago you might have agreed that the chance his story would end up in this book was not great. His nickname in the community was "Big Bad Jim from Bell Creek." For starters, the old Jim was drug-dependent, and an alcoholic. There was a fifteen-year period in his life when he was seldom sober. And he tells of many opportunities he had to get acquainted with the interior of the county jail.

But let me back up just a little. Jim is an RN and had a good job in charge in the Intensive Care Unit in a large metropolitan hospital in an adjoining community. But because of alcohol and methamphetamines, he began a downward spiral that would nearly cost him his life.

He became involved in the drug world, quit his job, and thought he'd make a fortune dealing drugs.

But, as he says, he soon discovered that wasn't a safe way to make a living. Some of his friends were killed. Others ended up doing long sentences in prison. And he watched as drugs took a catastrophic toll on his friends who were users.

In an unusual turn of events, Jim met a young woman who had a Seventh-day Adventist background. They often had intense arguments about topics from the Bible, but she seemed to have the ability to "win."

God was finally able to help Jim see that life had more to offer than he was finding. God miraculously took the alcoholic addiction away, then he delivered Jim from his addiction to drugs.

Reflecting on his Bible arguments with his girl friend, Jim headed for the closest Seventh-day Adventist church. She wanted nothing to do with him if he was going to go straight, so he lost a girl friend, but he gained a church family.

God not only dramatically changed Jim's appetites and goals but also his attitude. Instead of taking advantage of people and heading them down a one-way road to misery, he began to talk to them about life—eternal life.

Another dramatic change in Jim's life involved his family. For instance, usually the Christmas holidays were controlled by alcohol and that meant everyone was going to be drinking for three days with all the distress and bad feelings that go with it. But this first Christmas after his conversion was different. Knowing Jim as they did, they were certain the story of his "change" couldn't be true.

Apparently Jim's influence in his own family is greater than he knew. When he was completely sober throughout the holidays, they watched him, and then an incredible thing happened—none of them would touch alcohol either! "It was the first really happy Christmas in our family that any of us could remember," Jim would later say.

His mother and other family members come to church with him now when they can. It's obvious to them that the stories are true, and they want to know why Jim is so changed.

Because many of the people at the local jail were his friends, Jim went there—on the other side of the bars this time—to talk to them about what he had found. The transformation in his life was so real, so evident, that no one had reason to ques-tion it.

Big Bad Jim

Jim felt called again to a hos-pital setting, this time for ministry. The Lord seemed to be calling him there, but he wasn't sure for what. One day Jim drove to a hospital some 60 miles from his home. He parked his car in the parking lot and prayed that the Lord would guide him to some patient or some family who needed him.

He entered the hospital waiting room where families and friends wait for their loved ones to come back from surgery. As he sat there he prayed silently for the people who were there and for the patients they were waiting for. Nothing dramatic happened.

The next day he drove back. God seemed to have some specific purpose in mind, but Jim still wasn't sure what it was. In the waiting area, there was a large group of people, but they all seemed to be engrossed in their own circumstances. So he went to the waiting room on the surgical unit.

This time there was a couple, perhaps in their 50's, who sat over in the corner obviously in a deep discussion, and he overheard enough of their conversation that he could sense their distress. Jim approached and asked if there was any way he could be of help.

They explained to him that they were facing some very serious medical decisions. The surgery the husband so desperately needed could be life-threatening, but not to have it could be, too.

After they had talked together for several minutes, Jim prayed with them. All of them were weeping when he finished. He could sense that there were not three in the room, but four, and because Jim had been faithful to God's call, God Himself was true to His promise to be present. Before Jim left, his new-found friends assured him they had found hope and the beginning of peace.

It's not "Big, Bad Jim from Bell Creek" any more. No. Now you might recognize him as "That gentle bridge-builder from Bell Creek."

Ron and Jelaine are also bridge builders. Jelaine is an RN and Ron is a Physical Therapist. Ron is also the "sweet singer in Israel" in our church.

They are constantly on the lookout for ways they can be of help. You might find them doing some "low-tech" bridge building, like walking a dog for a shut-in neighbor.

While working with a patient in Rehabilitation one Sunday, the thought came to Ron—almost an urgent thought—"Sing to this lady."

Though Ron has studied voice, has a rich musical gift, and has sung in public for years, he now found himself in unfamiliar territory. But the thought of her need seemed pressing, so he began to sing,

> *Amazing Grace, shall always be my song of praise.*
> *For it was grace that bought my liberty.*
> *I do not know just why He came to love me so,*
> *He looked beyond my fault and saw my need."*
> Dottie Rambo

It must have been the exact message God wanted her to hear. The patient was obviously moved by the message. Later he overheard her say to another patient, "Ask him; you must hear this song, too!"

So Ron sang the song twice that day, giving the Holy Spirit rich avenues to reach hearts with God's amazing grace. Here were two people reached by the God of heaven with a message that God doesn't focus on our faults, but rather sees our every need.

Singing in Rehab? Now there's an unusual bridge. But God has plans for all kinds of Kingdom-bridges He wants His people to build.

Ron also studies the Bible with an attending non-member, Renee. She's part of our church family and we love her. You might see Ron in Renee's yard, cutting the grass, or helping with some other landscape project when Renee needs extra help.

Ron and Jelaine are in the bridge-building business.

And so is Sadie.

What makes Sadie so special? Sadie has cultivated and fine-tuned her gift of kindness. She always notices when someone is absent from church; she phones and visits or sends a card. People love it.

Sadie is a wonderful greeter in our church because she is there with a hug and a bulletin. Oh, and did I mention a warm smile?

Sadie also visits the jail, and there is at least one member in our church today who will tell you he is there because Sadie came regularly to the county jail to visit him.

Our young energetic pastor, David Wright, is what our granddaughter, Abigail, would call a "with it" pastor. He's known in the community as a helper, and has established strong personal relationships with other pastors in town. A few weeks ago, as a result of his participation in a Good Friday service, a local Lutheran pastor visited our church and worshiped with us.

Pastor Dave creates the climate and leads the way so members and leaders of other faith groups in our community will see us as warm, caring people who love Jesus. He's teaching us to be bridge builders.

Look around you. Who in your church is building bridges? Could they use some help? What can you learn from them? There are people in every church who are known in the community because they are friendly, accepting, and willing helpers. Watch them; attitudes are contagious.

Some compelling reasons to become certified Kingdom bridge builders, eager to show God's love in practical ways:

1. That's what Christians do. That's what Christ has asked us to do—simple things, but significant. It's not an option; it's a privilege.

2. It enriches our own journey when we serve others. This is the way God intended that our faith should work. When we help someone else up the mountain, we get closer to the top ourselves.

3. It's part of the message of the kingdom. We're not just a "proclaiming" church, we're also called to be a "healing" church.

4. It helps us learn to see as God sees. God never tires of showing mercy and kindness. Responding to His nudging that we show kindness gives us opportunity to learn to look through His eyes at the people He loves.

5. It demonstrates to the world around us that we really are followers of Christ. We never know who may be watching, but many want to know if Christians are for real, and more importantly, if God is for real. Our actions help the skeptical to see authenticity.

What I've just described is not about technical, heavy-duty skills reserved for the highly-gifted. It's simple examples of how we can demonstrate His love when we have "the mind of Christ." We are instructed as we bathe ourselves in His Word, we are sensitized as we ask Him to bring people to us we can love, and we are energized as we plead for His in-filling.

He rejoices to use us to build bridges of hope to the hopeless, help to the helpless, joy to the joyless, peace to the distressed, love to the unloved.

You can *do* this.

Epilogue

You can *do* this.

Other books by the Jacobsens:

By Ruthie Jacobsen:

- God Wants to Hear You Sing
- Prayer, a Still Place In the Storm
- Kneeling on the Promises
- The Difference is Prayer
- A Passion for Prayer
  (co-authored with Lonnie Melashenko & Tim Crosby)
- Because You Prayed (co-authored with Penny Estes Wheeler)
- Putting Their Hands In His; Teaching Children to Pray
- Do It the Right Way

By Don Jacobsen:

- Call to Joy
- Battle For the Mind

The authors may be contacted at:

ruthiej@earthlink.net

or

1donj@earthlink.net

Our pumpkin man
smiles back at us
with a happy,
glowing face.

put the pumpkin
head in place.

We go outside
at sunset,

We draw a face
and cut it out.
A light is all it needs.

We cut the top
to get inside.
We scoop out
all the seeds.

We find the best of all!

Pumpkins

We look around
the pumpkin patch.

Some are bumpy.
Some are small.

Some are short
and some are tall.

It's time to pick
a pumpkin head.
We'll find the
nicest one.

We give him gloves.
We give him boots.
We're having so much fun.

We fill and stuff the body
with lots of crunchy leaves.

We button all the buttons.
We tie up legs and sleeves.

We run inside
and find old clothes.

We'll make a pumpkin man.

What can we do
with all these leaves?
I know. I have a plan.

We jump on top.
We toss them up
and watch the colors fly.

We go outside.
We rake the leaves.
We pile them way up high.

THE PUMPKIN MAN

by Judith Moffatt

Hello Reader! — Level 2

SCHOLASTIC INC.

Cartwheel
·B·O·O·K·S·®

New York Toronto London Auckland Sydney

To Emma and Sam,
and to my dad, who helped
me make my first pumpkin man
— J.M.

Cut-paper photography by Paul Dyer

Copyright © 1998 by Judith Moffatt.
All rights reserved. Published by Scholastic Inc.
SCHOLASTIC, HELLO READER!, CARTWHEEL BOOKS and associated logos
are trademarks and/or registered trademarks of Scholastic Inc.

Library of Congress Cataloging-in-Publication Data
Moffatt, Judith.
    The pumpkin man / by Judith Moffatt.
        p.   cm. — (Hello reader! Level 2)
    "Cartwheel books."
    Summary: Children stuff old clothes with autumn leaves, add gloves
and boots and a carved pumpkin head with a light inside, and thus make a
pumpkin man with a happy glowing face. Includes instructions for making a
pumpkin man.
        ISBN 0-590-63865-3
        [1. Pumpkin—Fiction.   2. Jack-o'-lanterns—Fiction.   3. Stories in rhyme.]
    I. Title. II. Series.
    PZ8.3.M716Pu   1998
    [E]—dc21   98-21324
                                                                                 CIP
                                                                                  AC
        12   11   10 9   8   03

                            Printed in the U.S.A.   23
                        First printing, October 1998

Hello, Family Members,

Learning to read is one of the most im~~~ of early childhood. **Hello Reader!** boc children become skilled readers who ..... readers learn to read by remembering frequently used wo~~ like "the," "is," and "and"; by using phonics skills to decode new words; and by interpreting picture and text clues. These books provide both the stories children enjoy and the structure they need to read fluently and independently. Here are suggestions for helping your child *before*, *during*, and *after* reading:

Before

- Look at the cover and pictures and have your child predict what the story is about.
- Read the story to your child.
- Encourage your child to chime in with familiar words and phrases.
- Echo read with your child by reading a line first and having your child read it after you do.

During

- Have your child think about a word he or she does not recognize right away. Provide hints such as "Let's see if we know the sounds" and "Have we read other words like this one?"
- Encourage your child to use phonics skills to sound out new words.
- Provide the word for your child when more assistance is needed so that he or she does not struggle and the experience of reading with you is a positive one.
- Encourage your child to have fun by reading with a lot of expression . . . like an actor!

After

- Have your child keep lists of interesting and favorite words.
- Encourage your child to read the books over and over again. Have him or her read to brothers, sisters, grandparents, and even teddy bears. Repeated readings develop confidence in young readers.
- Talk about the stories. Ask and answer questions. Share ideas about the funniest and most interesting characters and events in the stories.

I do hope that you and your child enjoy this book.

— Francie Alexander
Reading Specialist,
Scholastic's Instructional Publishing Group

Level G